Play With Me

Robin shrugged. "Both sound like fun."

"Well, I want to play tag," Elizabeth said.

"Jump rope," Jessica said.

"Tag," Elizabeth said.

"Come on, you two," Robin pleaded. "It's no big deal."

"Right," Elizabeth said. "So let's play tag."

Jessica stomped her foot. "No! That's not fair."

Amy ran up. "Does anyone want to play on the swings? There are two open."

Robin smiled at Amy. "I love swings. See you guys later!"

Elizabeth and Jessica watched as their cousin ran off with Amy.

"Thanks a lot, Jessica," Elizabeth said. "Now look what you've done."

"Me?" Jessica said. "It's all *your* fault."

The twins glared at each other.

Bantam Books in the SWEET VALLEY KIDS series

SWEET VALLEY KIDS

ROBIN
IN THE
MIDDLE

Written by
Molly Mia Stewart

Created by
FRANCINE PASCAL

Illustrated by
Ying-Hwa Hu

A BANTAM BOOK®
NEW YORK · TORONTO · LONDON · SYDNEY · AUCKLAND

RL 2, 005-008

ROBIN IN THE MIDDLE
A Bantam Skylark Book / July 1993

Sweet Valley High® and Sweet Valley Kids are
trademarks of Francine Pascal

Conceived by Francine Pascal

Produced by Daniel Weiss Associates, Inc.
33 West 17th Street
New York, NY 10011

Cover art by Susan Tang

ISBN: 0-553-48014-6

Published simultaneously in the United States and Canada

PRINTED IN THE UNITED STATES OF AMERICA

CWO   0 9 8 7 6 5 4 3 2

ROBIN
IN THE
MIDDLE

CHAPTER 1

Visitors

"I found the bag of balloons," Elizabeth Wakefield said after school on Friday. She crawled out from under her twin sister, Jessica's, bed and blew a dust ball off her nose.

"Good," Jessica Wakefield said. She closed the desk drawer where she had been looking and plopped down on the floor. "Can I have one?"

Elizabeth handed Jessica a green balloon.

"No, I want a pink one," Jessica said. Pink was her favorite color.

Elizabeth laughed. "OK, I'll take the green

·

one. Now let's see who blows hers up faster."

The girls quickly blew up their balloons. They finished at exactly the same time. That wasn't surprising, because Jessica and Elizabeth were identical twins. They often said the same thing at the same time, and whenever they paired off in a three-legged race, they always won. Nothing could trip them up, because their timing was perfect.

Elizabeth and Jessica looked exactly alike too. They both had blue-green eyes and long blond hair with bangs. The girls often wore the same outfits, but Elizabeth liked most of her clothes to be green, while Jessica usually chose pink.

The twins were different in other ways too. Elizabeth liked reading and writing stories. She spent a lot of time outside playing soccer and other sports.

Jessica was just the opposite. She liked to stay inside to play with her dolls and dollhouse. When Jessica did go outdoors, she didn't play games that would mess up her clothes. She preferred safe games like jump rope and hopscotch.

"Whew," Jessica said a few minutes later. She and Elizabeth had each finished blowing up four balloons. "I think we have enough."

Elizabeth agreed, so they quickly gathered up the balloons and ran downstairs. In the kitchen, they got a roll of string. Then they rushed outside and tied the balloons to the lamppost in front of their house.

"Now Robin and Uncle Kirk and Aunt Nancy will remember where we live," Elizabeth said.

Jessica bounced up and down. "They should be here any second."

Robin was the twins' cousin. She and her parents were driving down from San Francisco for a weekend visit. Robin was almost the same age as Jessica and Elizabeth. She was one of their favorite cousins.

Mrs. Wakefield came outside. "The balloons

look great, girls. I'm glad you thought of hanging them."

"We don't want Robin to get lost," Jessica said.

"Don't forget Stacey," Mrs. Wakefield reminded them. Stacey was Robin's younger sister, and she was coming too.

"Oops!" Elizabeth said, putting her hand over her mouth. "How old is Stacey now?"

Mrs. Wakefield thought for a minute. "She should be three years old now."

Just then the phone rang inside.

Mrs. Wakefield turned toward the door. "I'd better get that. Maybe our visitors are lost."

"I guess Stacey will have to stay in our room too," Jessica said as she watched her mother go. "What a drag. She's just a baby."

"We'll still have fun," Elizabeth said.

"Absolutely," Jessica agreed. "The first thing I'm going to do is show Robin my dollhouse."

"We can play with it for a little while," Elizabeth said. "But then I want to play soccer. Todd taught me how to hit a head ball. I've got to show Robin that." Todd Wilkins and Elizabeth were teammates on the Sweet Valley Soccer League.

"How do you know Robin even likes soccer?" Jessica asked.

"How do you know she likes dolls?" Elizabeth countered.

Jessica frowned. "She liked them last time she visited."

"I remember," Elizabeth admitted. "But that was a long time ago."

Jessica bit her lip. "We were in first grade then."

Suddenly Elizabeth wasn't so sure how the visit would go. She and Jessica had changed a lot since the last time they had seen Robin.

Jessica must have been thinking the same thing. "You don't think Robin will be too

5

different, do you?" she asked.

"I don't know," Elizabeth said. "But we're about to find out."

A green station wagon pulled into the Wakefields' driveway. Aunt Nancy was driving. Uncle Kirk was sitting in the front seat, holding a map. Robin and Stacey were waving from the backseat.

"They're here," Jessica said, looking a little worried.

Elizabeth grabbed her sister's hand and squeezed it. She was worried too.

CHAPTER 2

A Great Pen

Robin jumped out of the station wagon as soon as it stopped. "Hi, Jess!" she yelled. "Hi, Liz!"

Stacey crawled across the car seat and out the door her sister had opened. "Hi, Jess!" she yelled. "Hi, Liz!"

Robin rolled her eyes. "Stacey does everything I do."

Stacey pouted. "I do not!"

"You look just like you did the last time we saw you," Elizabeth told Robin.

"Like us," Jessica added.

Robin had chin-length blond hair and blue

eyes. She wasn't as tall as the twins, but she *did* look a lot like them. Stacey looked very different. She had freckles, and red hair that she wore in pigtails.

Aunt Nancy and Uncle Kirk got out of the car.

"Hi, girls," Aunt Nancy called out. "Come give me a hug!"

"Me, too," Uncle Kirk said.

Jessica and Elizabeth ran over and gave their aunt and uncle each a hug.

"You two have each grown a foot since the last time we saw you," Aunt Nancy told them.

Jessica looked down at the ground. "We did? I don't feel any taller."

"Well, believe it," Uncle Kirk said. "Your mom and dad must be feeding you fertilizer."

Elizabeth laughed. "We're not as tall as *you*, Uncle Kirk."

Uncle Kirk was unusually tall. He had curly red hair, like Stacey. Aunt Nancy was Mrs. Wakefield's sister. She had blond hair and blue eyes, just like the twins' mom.

"Hi, Nancy. Hi, Kirk," Mrs. Wakefield called out from the doorway. "I'm glad you made it."

The twins' older brother, Steven, came out of the house after Mrs. Wakefield. He was two years older than Jessica and Elizabeth— and he never let them forget it. Steven's favorite thing to do was tease the twins. His second favorite thing to do was play tricks on them. His third favorite thing to do was make fun of them.

"Hi, Steven," Robin said.

"Hi, Steven," Stacey said.

"Hi," Steven said back. He shook his head. "Mom, can I go to my room? There are too many girls around here."

Mrs. Wakefield frowned. "That's not a very nice way to welcome your cousins."

"Please," Steven begged.

Mrs. Wakefield laughed. "OK, go."

Steven ran back inside.

"Let me help you get your suitcases inside," Mrs. Wakefield told Aunt Nancy and Uncle Kirk. The grown-ups started getting bags out of the car.

Stacey tugged on Jessica's T-shirt. "Do you want to see my doll? Her name is Matilda."

Robin wrinkled her nose. "That's Stacey's favorite doll. She takes it everywhere."

Stacey held the baby doll up as high as she could, trying to hand it to Jessica. The doll was naked, a bit dirty, and her hair was in knots.

"Hey, I have a doll just like this!" Jessica said, taking Matilda from Stacey. Then she turned pink. "Elizabeth and I used to play with it when we were little," she added.

"Kids, give us a hand getting the car unpacked," Uncle Kirk called out.

The twins grabbed Robin's and Stacey's bags out of the trunk and carried them up to their room. Then Jessica searched through a big pile of stuff in her side of the closet. She pulled out a doll that was identical to Matilda.

"See?" Jessica said, showing the doll to Stacey. "My doll matches Matilda. Her name is Suzanne."

"Wow," Stacey said, reaching for the doll. "I can pretend Matilda and Suzanne are twins. Just like you and Elizabeth."

The girls laughed.

"I brought you presents," Robin announced. She pulled two packages out of her suitcase and handed them to the twins.

Jessica unwrapped a pink satin hair ribbon. Elizabeth got a cool comic book.

"Thanks!" Elizabeth and Jessica said.

"You forgot," Stacey said. She pulled another present out of Robin's suitcase.

"I didn't forget," Robin said. "That's for Steven."

"Why did you bring a present for Steven?" Elizabeth asked.

"You'll see," Robin said.

Jessica and Elizabeth exchanged smiles. They could tell that Robin was up to something.

"Let's see *now*," Jessica said.

Robin and the twins ran to Steven's room and pounded on his door. Stacey followed them, carrying Matilda and Suzanne.

"What do you want?" Steven called out. "Don't you see the NO TRESPASSING sign hanging on the door?"

"Robin brought you a present," Elizabeth yelled back.

"Oh, OK. Come in," Steven said right away.

Robin pushed open the door and handed Steven the small package. Steven ripped the paper off.

"It's a pen," Steven said, sounding disappointed. He turned it around in his hand. "Uh, thanks, Robin."

Robin smiled. "You're welcome. Why don't you try it? It's got bright purple ink."

13

Steven took the pen cap off. Ink squirted out all over him. He threw the pen on the floor. "Thanks a lot!" he yelled as a huge purple blotch appeared on his white T-shirt. "You ruined my favorite T-shirt."

Robin frowned. "What did I do? There's nothing to get upset about."

"Yes, there is. That stupid pen squirted ink all over me," Steven shouted.

"Where?" Robin asked.

"Can't you see?" Steven yelled. "Right he—" But when he looked down at his shirt, the spot was gone.

"What—" Steven whispered.

Robin started to giggle. Elizabeth and Jessica joined in.

"What's so funny?" Stacey demanded.

"It's disappearing ink," Robin blurted out. "Got you, Steven."

Steven's face turned red. "Get out of my room!"

Laughing, the girls ran back to the twins'

room and fell onto Jessica's bed.

"I'm really glad you're here," Elizabeth told Robin.

Jessica smiled. She was glad too. This was going to be a terrific weekend.

CHAPTER 3

Another Joke

"You made Steven really mad," Elizabeth told Robin.

"Yeah," Jessica said. "It was great."

"Jess!" Elizabeth said.

"You laughed too," Jessica reminded her sister.

"It *was* funny," Elizabeth admitted.

Robin smiled. "I'm great at thinking up jokes."

"Mom says you think up too many jokes," Stacey put in. She looked from Jessica to Elizabeth. "Robin gets in trouble a lot."

"That's not true," Robin defended herself. "It's not that often."

"Just last week—" Stacey said.

Robin sighed. "Stacey, I think I hear Mom calling you."

"I didn't hear—" Elizabeth started to say, but Robin pinched her. "Oh, yeah, I hear Aunt Nancy calling too."

Stacey frowned. She looked as if she knew the older girls were trying to fool her.

"You'd better hurry," Jessica told Stacey. "*You* don't want to get in trouble, do you?"

"Nooo," Stacey said. She got up and walked slowly toward the stairs, dragging Matilda and Suzanne after her.

"I don't get in trouble that often," Robin said firmly.

"What have you ever done?" Jessica asked.

"Once I put glue on the piano keys at school," Robin said. "And once I put a tack on a boy's chair—but the teacher sat on it instead."

Jessica laughed. "Can you think of another trick for us to play on Steven?"

"He's always teasing us," Elizabeth explained.

"Sure," Robin said. "What does he like to do?"

"Play basketball," Elizabeth said.

"Ride his bike," Jessica added.

"Eat," Elizabeth said. "And eat and eat."

"Let me think," Robin said. A second later, she leaned forward and whispered, "OK, here's what we'll do . . ."

By the time Robin had finished explaining her plan, the twins were both smiling.

"You *are* good at thinking up tricks," Elizabeth said.

"Come on," Jessica said. "Let's try it."

Robin and the twins tiptoed down to the Wakefields' garage. Mr. and Mrs. Wakefield's station wagon was parked inside.

"There's Steven's bike," Jessica whispered as she pointed to the side of the garage.

19

While Robin went over to the bike, Jessica and Elizabeth searched through a pile of tools. About two minutes later, the girls opened the car door and got inside. They kneeled down on the floor where nobody could see them. Then they waited. And waited. And waited.

"He's not coming," Elizabeth said.

"Maybe we should give up," Jessica agreed. "My legs are cramped."

"Shh," Robin whispered. "I hear footsteps."

Sure enough, Steven walked into the garage and got on his bike. As soon as he sat down, Steven realized something was wrong. He got off the bike and examined it.

"The tire's flat," Steven mumbled. "How did that happen?"

"I let the air out," Robin whispered so only the twins could hear.

Jessica started to giggle. She clapped her hand over her mouth just in time.

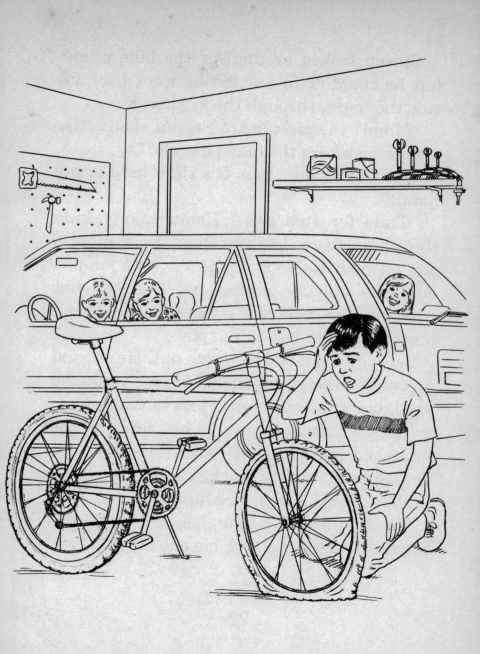

Steven looked around for the bike pump, but he couldn't find it. So he went back inside the house through the kitchen.

"Mom!" the girls heard Steven shout. "Do you know where the bike pump is?"

Jessica giggled. "I do. It's right here in my hand."

"Time for step two," Robin said, taking the pump from Jessica. Quiet as a mouse, she opened the door of the car and jumped out. She quickly pumped up Steven's flat front tire. As soon as she was finished, Robin hurried back to her hiding place.

Seconds later, Steven came out. He started to look for the pump again. After a while, he went over to have another look at the tire.

"That's really weird," he said as he scratched his head. "It looks fine now." He headed back into the kitchen.

"Mom!" the girls heard him yell.

"He's probably telling her he's leaving," Elizabeth whispered. "We have to hurry."

Again Robin snuck out of the car. This time she let the air out of Steven's back tire.

When Steven came back, he was whistling. He jumped on his bike and began to pedal. The frame of his back tire scraped against the concrete. Steven stopped whistling. He looked at his tire and saw that it was completely flat.

Elizabeth ducked her head down as she burst into laughter.

Steven jumped off his bike, ran toward the car, and threw the door open.

"I'm getting sick of you guys," Steven shouted at Robin, Elizabeth, and Jessica. "Your jokes are so funny, I'm going to laugh all the way to the park." Then he slammed the car door.

"That was perfect," Robin said.

"We really got him," Jessica agreed.

"I can't wait to do it again," Elizabeth said, smiling. "And soon."

CHAPTER 4

Trick Number Three

On their way in from the garage, Jessica, Elizabeth, and Robin stopped in the kitchen. Mrs. Wakefield and Robin's mother and father were all there talking.

"What have you been doing?" Mrs. Wakefield asked. "You've been awfully quiet."

Robin hid a smile. "Nothing special. Just having fun."

Uncle Kirk winked. "Sounds like mischief to me."

"What are we having for dinner tonight?" Jessica asked. She wanted to change the subject.

"Hamburgers," Uncle Kirk said. "On the barbecue."

"Yummy," Jessica said.

"Your dad will be home soon," Mrs. Wakefield told the twins. "We'll eat as soon as he gets here, so don't go far."

"And don't start making noise now," Aunt Nancy added. "Stacey is taking a nap."

"OK," Elizabeth said. "We'll be upstairs."

"Hamburgers are perfect for Trick Number Three," Robin whispered as they climbed the stairs.

"All right!" Jessica said. "Tell us."

"Daddy's home!" Elizabeth yelled a while later.

Mr. Wakefield had just come into the twins' room.

"Hi, Uncle Ned," Robin greeted him.

"Hello, Robin." Mr. Wakefield gave her a big hug and kiss. "How are you?"

"Hungry," Robin said.

Mr. Wakefield laughed. "Good! I came to tell you it's dinnertime. Come on outside."

The girls followed Mr. Wakefield downstairs. But they stopped when they got to the kitchen.

"We'll be out in a minute," Jessica told her dad.

"Right," Elizabeth said. "We have to, uh—"

"Wash our hands," Robin put in.

"OK, but hurry," Mr. Wakefield said. "The hamburgers are almost ready."

As soon as Mr. Wakefield had walked outside, Jessica pulled a jar out of the refrigerator and handed it to her cousin. Robin opened the jar and smelled the red stuff that was inside.

"Will it work?" Jessica asked.

"It's perfect," Robin announced.

Elizabeth looked worried. "I'm not sure we should do this."

"You liked the other jokes," Jessica reminded

her. "You wanted to play another one."

"This is different," Elizabeth said. "What if we hurt Steven?"

"We won't." Robin sighed. "Now go."

Jessica led the way outside. When nobody was looking, Robin poured a tablespoon of the red sauce onto a hamburger. Jessica slipped the hamburger onto a plate.

"Here's one for you," Jessica told her brother.

"Great," Steven said. "I'm starved."

Steven didn't pay any attention to the red sauce oozing out from under the bun. It looked just like ketchup. But as soon as he took a huge bite of the hamburger and started to chew, his eyes bugged out. Tears ran down his face.

"Water," Steven said gasping. "Soda, iced tea. Help!"

Jessica and Robin started to giggle.

Elizabeth quickly handed Steven a glass of iced tea.

"What's the matter, Steven?" Mrs. Wakefield asked, rushing over.

Steven drank the entire glass of tea. Then he took a deep breath. "My hamburger is poisoned," he shrieked. "I almost died."

"Let me try it." Mrs. Wakefield took the rest of the hamburger from Steven.

"No!" Robin, Jessica, and Elizabeth all yelled.

"What's going on?" Uncle Kirk asked. "Girls?"

"We put hot sauce on Steven's hamburger," Elizabeth said.

Jessica laughed. "You should have seen your face!"

"I guess it was a real mouthful," Robin added.

"Wait until I get back at all of you," Steven fumed. "You'll know what a joke really is then."

"Now, now," Uncle Kirk said. "There'll be no more pranks, jokes, or tricks." He looked at Robin. "Isn't that right?"

"Yes, Dad," Robin said. "I'm sorry."

"Good." Mrs. Wakefield threw the "poisoned" hamburger in the trash and gave Steven a new one. "I think you'll survive, honey."

"I guess," Steven said. But he sounded grumpy.

"We have our own Three Musketeers," Uncle Kirk said, flipping the last burgers over on the barbecue grill.

"What's a musketeer?" Elizabeth asked.

"A kind of soldier," Mrs. Wakefield explained. "The Three Musketeers were friends who went everywhere together."

"They had a motto," Mr. Wakefield said. "It was 'All for one and one for all'."

"And they got into a lot of trouble," Aunt Nancy added.

"Are we in trouble?" Jessica asked.

Mrs. Wakefield thought for a second. "No, but I think you've teased Steven enough.

Promise to give him a break from now on."

"OK," Elizabeth, Jessica, and Robin answered together.

Robin grinned. "The Three Musketeers."

"That's us," Elizabeth said.

"Best friends forever," Jessica said. *Robin's great,* she told herself. *She's even more fun than Elizabeth. Elizabeth hardly ever plays jokes.*

CHAPTER 5

Mud Fight

"If we can't play any more tricks," Robin asked after they'd finished eating, "what can we do?"

"Let's go kick my soccer ball around," Elizabeth suggested.

"I have a better idea," Jessica said. "Let's play with my dollhouse."

"What do you want to do?" Elizabeth asked Robin. "You're the guest."

Robin shrugged her shoulders. "It doesn't matter to me."

"Then why don't we go to the park first?" Elizabeth said. "We can play dolls later." She looked at Jessica. "Is that OK?"

Jessica hesitated. "I guess so," she finally said.

"Great." Elizabeth smiled and went to get her soccer ball.

"We're going to the park," Robin called out to her father.

"Be back in an hour," Uncle Kirk called back. "It'll be dark soon."

"Don't worry," Jessica mumbled. "I hope we're back sooner."

"I might join a soccer team at home," Robin told the twins as they started to walk to the park.

"I play on the Sweet Valley Soccer League after school," Elizabeth said. "It's a lot of fun. You have to be quick on your feet."

"Are you on the team too?" Robin asked Jessica.

"No," Jessica said. "I don't like soccer."

"I just started to play," Robin said. "But I

don't know the rules or anything."

"Then I'll teach you," Elizabeth offered.

When they reached the park, Elizabeth showed Robin how to dribble the ball using the instep of each foot, how to pass to another player, and how to kick it for a goal. She was proud to know so much.

"This is neat," Robin said as she practiced controlling the ball all the way to the playing field.

The field was all muddy.

"It rained last night," Elizabeth explained to Robin.

"I don't think we can play," Jessica said. "We'll sink into the mud."

But Robin ran right onto the field. "Come on. The mud will make it more fun. Pass me the ball, Liz!"

Elizabeth kicked the ball, along with a big clump of mud. The ball landed in front of Robin, and the clump of mud hit her right in the middle of the forehead.

"Eww," Jessica said. "Gross! I knew we'd get dirty."

"Sorry," Elizabeth called out. "I didn't mean to—"

Robin ran toward her. She was grinning. "I'm going to get you for that!" When she got close to Elizabeth, she scooped up a handful of mud, aimed, and threw it.

Elizabeth turned and tried to run away. *Thwack!* The mud hit her right on the back. Elizabeth sank down onto her knees. She looked as if she were crying.

"Liz, are you OK?" Jessica called out.

Elizabeth didn't answer.

Robin ran up behind Elizabeth. "Please don't cry. I didn't mean to hurt you."

In a flash, Elizabeth grabbed a handful of mud, spun around, and smeared it onto Robin's shirt. "Got you!"

The fight was on! Robin attacked Elizabeth, and Elizabeth attacked Robin until they were both covered in mud. Only Jessica stood

on the side of the field, watching.

"Come on, Jess," Robin yelled. "This is great. You'll love it!"

"No way. I don't want to get dirty," Jessica said.

"Let's get her," Robin whispered to Elizabeth.

Each girl grabbed two handfuls of mud and started to walk toward Jessica.

Jessica took a step backward. "Two against one—no fair!"

"Too bad," Robin sang out. She threw a handful of mud and missed. Jessica started to run, but when she turned back to see if anyone was close to her, Robin threw another handful and hit Jessica in the chest.

Jessica stopped. "Yuck!" Just then more mud hit Jessica's bare leg. "Liz!"

Elizabeth and Robin laughed, but Jessica looked angry.

Robin's great, Elizabeth told herself. *She's more fun than Jessica. Jessica never likes to play messy games.*

CHAPTER 6

Left Out

"My goodness, what happened to you?" Aunt Nancy asked.

"You look like monsters," Stacey said.

When Robin and the twins got back from the park, their parents were sitting in the Wakefields' backyard. Stacey was curled up on Uncle Kirk's lap. She was wearing pajamas with feet on them.

Elizabeth grinned. "We had a mud fight at the park."

"It looks more like a mud war to me," Mrs. Wakefield said, laughing. She shook her head. "I don't know how we're going to get you clean without getting the entire house dirty."

"The mud's drying," Robin said. "See, it's cracking off. Then we'll be clean."

Elizabeth and Robin exchanged smiles. Jessica didn't know what they were so happy about. Every inch of her body felt dirty. All she wanted was to take a nice hot bath.

"Why don't we hose them off?" Uncle Kirk suggested.

"That's a great idea, but we can do it ourselves," Robin said. "Where's the hose?"

"I'll show you," Elizabeth said.

Robin and Elizabeth ran off to the side of the house.

Jessica didn't follow. She crossed her arms across her chest. "There's no way I'm getting cold water all over me."

"Come on, Jessica. You should be laughing about this. If you hate the mud so much, the hose will get the worst of it off," Mrs. Wakefield said. "Afterward you can go upstairs and have a bath."

"Do I have to?" Jessica asked.

"Yes," Mrs. Wakefield said. "Unless you want to stay out here all night."

Jessica stomped off after Elizabeth and Robin. She found them squirting each other with the hose.

"If you guys get me, I'll be really mad," Jessica warned. "Don't even try it."

Robin handed her the hose. "I'm sorry I got you dirty."

"Yeah. Don't be mad," Elizabeth said. "We were just playing."

"I'm not mad," Jessica said. "I guess."

After hosing off, Elizabeth, Robin, and Jessica took turns taking baths. Then Mr. Wakefield announced that it was time for bed. The girls didn't have time to play dolls. Jessica was disappointed. She had been having fun with Robin before Elizabeth suggested they play soccer.

"You can sleep with me," Elizabeth told

Robin after the girls had brushed their teeth.

"Great," Robin said. "We can whisper under the covers."

Jessica's mouth dropped open. "That's not fair!"

"I'll sleep with you tomorrow," Robin said.

"OK," Jessica whispered. But she was upset.

Stacey crawled into Jessica's bed. "Come on, Jessica. You can sleep with me and Matilda and Suzanne."

"Great," Jessica mumbled as she got under the sheets.

"When I'm four, I get a big grown-up bed," Stacey said.

"Her birthday isn't for a long time," Robin added. "Stacey's a baby until then."

"But it's almost *your* birthday," Stacey said.

Elizabeth sat up. "Really, Robin?"

Robin nodded. "I'm going to be seven next week."

"That's great," Elizabeth said.

"Elizabeth and I are seven too," Jessica said.

"Are you going to have a party in San Francisco?" Elizabeth asked.

"Yes," Robin said. "I already sent out invitations. All of my friends are coming."

"We had a party too," Jessica said. "We ate pizzas and played sardines."

"Mom made us a cake," Elizabeth said.

Robin giggled. "We're getting my cake from the bakery. My mom isn't good at baking. Her cakes come out flat. But my dad makes great cookies."

"Maybe our mom can make you a cake while you're here," Jessica suggested.

"That sounds great," Elizabeth said. "We could give Robin a pre-birthday party."

Jessica smiled. Even though she was a little angry with Elizabeth, she wasn't mad at Robin. She was happy they were going to do something special for her cousin's birthday. And she was happy she had come up with the idea.

CHAPTER 7

Flip Flop

"Are you guys awake?" Robin asked the next morning.

"No," Elizabeth said, burying her head in her pillow.

"I am!" Jessica said. She popped up and looked around the room. "Hey, where's Stacey?"

"She always gets up really early," Robin said. "What should we do today?"

"Play with my dollhouse," Jessica said right away. "It's really, really fun. I have lots of furniture."

"OK," Robin said. "That's a good idea.

I love decorating all the rooms."

Jessica and Robin crawled out of bed and pulled the dollhouse away from the wall.

"Here's the mother," Jessica told Robin. "Here's the father. And look—I even have a dog and a cat."

Elizabeth sat up and watched them for a few minutes. She didn't feel like playing with the dollhouse. Elizabeth wanted to go outside.

"Aren't you guys going to get dressed?" Elizabeth asked, getting up.

"Not right now," Jessica said. She showed Robin a miniature wall mirror and dresser.

"Aren't you going to brush your teeth?" Elizabeth asked.

"No," Robin said.

"What about breakfast?" Elizabeth waited for a second, but Robin and Jessica didn't answer. So Elizabeth changed her clothes, brushed her teeth, and put her hair up in a ponytail. Then she went downstairs. Mrs.

Wakefield was in the kitchen, stirring a bowl of pancake batter. Aunt Nancy was slicing bananas.

"Hi, honey," Mrs. Wakefield said, giving Elizabeth a kiss on the forehead. "Where are Jessica and Robin?"

"Upstairs, playing with the dollhouse," Elizabeth answered. She took a banana slice and popped it in her mouth. "Mom, it's almost Robin's birthday. Jessica and I wanted to have a party."

"How nice," Aunt Nancy said. "Robin will be very spoiled this year."

"That's a great idea," Mrs. Wakefield agreed. "I'll tell you what—you and Jessica decide what you want to eat, and we'll have a special birthday dinner for Robin tonight."

"Thanks," Elizabeth said.

"Why don't you tell Jessica and Robin that breakfast is almost ready?" Aunt Nancy suggested.

Elizabeth sighed. "I don't think they'll come."

"Tell them we're making banana pancakes," Mrs. Wakefield said. "I bet that'll work."

"I'll try," Elizabeth agreed. She ran upstairs, feeling happy. She was looking forward to doing something special for Robin.

"Mom says to tell you breakfast is ready," Elizabeth said when she entered her bedroom. Jessica and Robin were lying on the floor in front of the dollhouse.

"I'm not hungry," Robin said, putting a miniature grandfather clock in the dollhouse's living room.

"It's banana pancakes," Elizabeth said.

Jessica sat up right away. She loved banana pancakes. "Maybe we should go. We can come back here after we eat."

Elizabeth bit her lip. She hoped that by the time breakfast was over, Jessica and Robin would forget about the dollhouse.

47

Then they could go to the park.

Robin ran downstairs in front of the twins.

"I told Mom about Robin's birthday," Elizabeth said to Jessica. "We're having a special dinner tonight. And you and I get to decide what we want to eat."

Jessica grinned. "Excellent!"

Robin, Jessica, and Elizabeth each gulped down a glass of orange juice and a glass of milk and ate a big stack of pancakes.

"I don't feel like playing with the doll-house anymore," Jessica announced after they finished eating.

Elizabeth smiled. Her wish was coming true.

"I want to play dress-up instead," Jessica said.

Elizabeth stuck out her tongue. But Robin grinned. "I love dress-up. Do you have a lot of clothes?"

"Yes," Jessica said. "I'll show you."

48

Jessica and Robin jumped up from their chairs and ran upstairs. Elizabeth followed them slowly. She didn't like playing with the dollhouse and she didn't like playing dress-up, either.

"I'm going to wear this," she heard Jessica tell Robin when she got upstairs. Jessica had opened their trunk of dress-up clothes and was pulling out a long, blue sequined dress.

"Ooo, it really sparkles," Robin said. She held up a yellow chiffon dress with a full skirt. "Look, this is beautiful. It's like a princess dress." Robin turned to Elizabeth. "What are you going to wear, Liz?"

Elizabeth sat down on her bed. "I don't care."

"What's the matter?" Robin asked.

"Nothing," Elizabeth muttered.

Jessica shrugged. She turned toward Robin. "I have some lipstick, too."

"Let me try some," Robin said.

Elizabeth yawned. Elizabeth sighed. But Robin and Jessica didn't notice. They were having too much fun.

Elizabeth couldn't believe Robin liked dolls. She couldn't believe Robin liked dress-up. She didn't understand why her cousin didn't want to be outside. After all, Robin liked to do what Elizabeth did. Didn't she?

CHAPTER 8

Squabbles

After lunch that day, Amy Sutton came over. She was in the twins' second-grade class and was one of Elizabeth's good friends. Jessica had suggested that Elizabeth call Amy and invite her over. She knew Amy liked to play outdoors, and hoped Elizabeth would stop bugging her and Robin if Amy was there.

"I'm glad you're here," Jessica told Amy. "This is my cousin, Robin."

"Robin, this is Amy, one of our friends from school," Elizabeth added.

"Hi, Robin," Amy said.

"Hi," Robin answered, smiling.

"Now we can go to the park," Elizabeth said. "Come on, Robin."

"No way," Jessica said. "I don't want to."

"But we played inside all morning," Elizabeth pointed out.

"I still haven't shown Robin my Barbie clothes," Jessica said.

"Robin's sick of your dolls," Elizabeth mumbled.

Jessica put her hands on her hips. "She is not!"

Amy glanced from Jessica to Elizabeth. She looked surprised.

Robin took Jessica's hand. "I know," she said. "How about if we play with Barbie after we get back from the park?"

Jessica frowned. "OK. I'll go if Robin wants to."

"Great," Elizabeth said. "I'll tell Mom."

A few minutes later, the girls were on their way.

"How old are you?" Amy asked Robin as they walked down the sidewalk.

"Six," Robin told her. "I'll be seven next week."

"We're having Robin's birthday dinner tonight," Elizabeth said. "The only thing we have to do is choose something really special to eat."

"I vote that we eat hamburgers," Jessica said.

"But we had hamburgers last night," Elizabeth said. "Robin doesn't want to eat them again."

Robin shrugged. "If everyone else wants hamburgers, it's all right with me."

"We do," Jessica said.

"We don't," Elizabeth said at the same time.

The twins gave each other angry looks.

Amy tried to change the subject. "I have an idea. Why don't you have root-beer floats?"

Jessica wrinkled her nose. "Yuck, I hate root beer."

"Yummy, I love root beer," Elizabeth said. "Root-beer floats sound great."

"You don't have to have them," Amy said. "It was just an idea."

"A terrible idea," Jessica mumbled.

Elizabeth stopped to face her sister. "There's no reason to make Amy feel bad. Anyway, this isn't your party, Jessica. It's Robin's. We're going to have what Robin likes."

Jessica turned to Robin. "You don't like root beer, either, do you?"

"I—" Robin started to say.

"Besides," Jessica went on. "We're going to have cake and ice cream. We can't have floats, too."

Elizabeth ignored Jessica. "Wait until you taste Mom's chocolate cake," she told Robin. "It's super-delicious."

"We're not having chocolate cake," Jessica

interrupted. "I want yellow cake with chocolate icing."

"Well, I want chocolate cake with white icing," Elizabeth said.

Robin cleared her throat loudly. "I like your socks, Amy."

"Thanks," Amy said. "I got them at the mall."

"Don't you like Amy's socks?" Robin asked the twins.

Jessica and Elizabeth didn't answer.

"Yellow cake is boring," Jessica finally said.

"You love yellow cake," Elizabeth said. "You just want to have everything your way."

"That's not true. I just want to have everything the *best* way," Jessica argued. "You're the one who's trying to ruin Robin's party." *But I'm going to stop you. I want Robin's party to be perfect, because Robin is one of my best friends. Maybe even my VERY best friend.*

CHAPTER 9

A Stand Off

Amy and Robin walked the rest of the way to the park together. Jessica and Elizabeth followed behind them, arguing.

"What's wrong with Elizabeth and Jessica?" Amy whispered to Robin.

"I don't know," Robin said. "At first we all had fun together. But then Jessica and Elizabeth started to fight." Robin looked at her sneakers. "I think it's my fault."

"It is not," Amy said. She patted Robin on the shoulder. "I bet they'll make up soon. They have to. They're best friends."

"I guess," Robin said.

"There's Eva." Amy pointed to Eva Simpson, who was in the same class as Amy and the twins. "I'll be right back." Amy ran toward the jungle gym.

Robin waited for her cousins to catch up to her. "This park is nice when it isn't muddy. What do you guys want to do?" she asked them.

"Let's play jump rope with Lila," Jessica said. Lila Fowler was one of Jessica's best friends from school.

"No," Elizabeth said. "Let's play tag with Todd and Kisho." Kisho Murasaki was a boy in the twins' class. Elizabeth played with him and Todd a lot.

Robin shrugged. "Both sound like fun."

Jessica faced Elizabeth with her arms crossed. "I don't want to play tag. I want to play jump rope."

"Well, I want to play tag," Elizabeth said.

"Jump rope," Jessica said.

"Tag," Elizabeth said.

Robin shifted her weight from one leg to the other. "Why don't we play tag, and then jump rope?" she said.

Elizabeth smiled. It was the second time Robin had put one of her suggestions before Jessica's. "Tag first sounds good to me."

"No way!" Jessica said.

"We could play jump rope first, and then tag," Robin offered. "I don't really care."

"Great," Jessica agreed.

"But the game will be over soon," Elizabeth complained.

"Too bad," Jessica said.

"Come on, you two," Robin pleaded. "It's not a big deal."

"Right," Elizabeth said. "So let's play tag."

Jessica stomped her foot. "No! That's not fair."

Amy ran up. "Does anyone want to play on the swings? There are two open."

"We're going to play tag," Elizabeth said

stubbornly. "Robin wants to."

"We're going to jump rope," Jessica said firmly.

Robin smiled at Amy. "I love swings. See you guys later!"

Elizabeth and Jessica watched Robin run off with Amy.

"Thanks a lot, Jessica," Elizabeth said. "Now look what you've done."

"Me?" Jessica said. "It's all *your* fault."

Elizabeth glared at her sister, but she didn't answer this time. She simply sat down next to a tree and leaned her back against it. Jessica sat down and leaned against the other side.

Kisho ran up to Elizabeth. "Are you going to play tag?"

"I don't feel like it anymore," Elizabeth said.

Kisho shrugged and ran off.

Lila came up to Jessica. "We need another person for jump rope. Do you want to play?"

"No!" Jessica said with a big frown.

"Fine," Lila said, walking off. She sounded mad.

A few minutes later, Robin walked up to the twins. She looked unhappy. "Why don't we just go back to your house? Amy is staying, but I'm not having much fun, and neither are you."

Without a word, Jessica and Elizabeth got up. Without a word, they started walking home.

"I don't understand," Elizabeth finally told Robin. "First you wanted to do everything I wanted to do. But then you started to play with Jessica."

"Yes," Jessica said. "Who do you like better—me or Elizabeth?"

"I like you both," Robin said. "Remember, we're the Three Musketeers."

Jessica shrugged. "I think they broke up."

CHAPTER 10

Stacey to the Rescue

Elizabeth lay down on her bed and opened a book.

Jessica sat down on her own bed. She picked up her stuffed koala and made it walk across the covers.

Robin looked from one twin to the other. They both looked grumpy. With a sigh, Robin sat down on the floor, where Stacey was playing with Matilda and Suzanne.

"Did you have a fight?" Stacey asked, breaking the stony silence.

Robin shook her head.

"Are you sad?" Stacey asked.

Robin nodded. She looked as if she were about to cry.

Stacey studied her sister for a minute. Then she pulled herself up and walked over to Jessica. "Here," Stacey said. "You can have Suzanne back now."

"Don't you want to play twins anymore?" Jessica asked.

"No," Stacey said.

"How come?" Jessica asked.

"Twins don't have any fun," Stacey answered.

"That's not true," Elizabeth said.

"Then why don't you play together?" Stacey asked.

No one answered.

Stacey stared at the twins for a long moment. Then she ran out of the room.

It got dark. But nobody called the girls for dinner. Jessica's stomach growled. She went downstairs to see what was happening with Robin's party. She found her parents and her aunt and uncle sitting around the kitchen table playing Scrabble. Stacey was playing with some blocks on the floor. Steven was watching television. No food was cooking. No decorations were hung.

"Aren't we celebrating Robin's birthday?" Jessica asked.

Mrs. Wakefield frowned. "I guess not. You and Elizabeth never told me what you wanted to eat."

Jessica's eyes widened. "But we *have* to have a party. We promised Robin."

Mrs. Wakefield shrugged. "As soon as you and your sister decide . . ."

Jessica had already turned toward the stairs. "I'll be right back!" she yelled as she ran up to her room. She got Elizabeth's attention and pulled her into the hallway. Elizabeth was upset when she heard what was happening. The twins ran down to the kitchen together.

"We want barbecued hamburgers," Jessica said. "I mean—is that OK, Liz?"

"Hamburgers sound good," Elizabeth said.

Mr. Wakefield frowned. "It's too late for a barbecue. How about spaghetti and meatballs?"

"OK," Elizabeth said.

Jessica nodded. "And we need a cake."

"What kind of cake?" Mrs. Wakefield asked.

"A birthday cake!" Elizabeth said.

Mrs. Wakefield went to the fridge and pulled out an angel-food cake. It said, "Happy Birthday, Robin" on top.

"How about this one?" Mrs. Wakefield asked.

Jessica and Elizabeth exchanged glances.

"You fooled us," Jessica said.

"That's right," Stacey said. "And it was *my* idea!"

Jessica and Elizabeth laughed. Then they ran upstairs to get Robin.

"Come on, Robin—" Jessica said.

"It's time for your birthday party!" Elizabeth said.

Robin looked from one twin to the other. "Did you guys make up?"

Elizabeth grinned. "Just because we both found a new friend—"

"Doesn't mean our old ones are less important," Jessica finished.

It was a terrific party. Elizabeth, Robin, and Jessica ate together and played together. The Three Musketeers were together again. All for one and one for all!

"Mom, we're bored," Jessica said on Sunday afternoon.

Mrs. Wakefield looked up from her paper and laughed. "How can you be bored? Your cousins have been gone for only an hour."

Elizabeth shrugged. "I don't know. We just are."

"You're not going to be bored for long,"

Mrs. Wakefield announced. "I'm taking the two of you on a trip."

"Really?" Elizabeth said.

"Just us?" Jessica asked.

"Just you and Elizabeth," Mrs. Wakefield said. "Your father and Steven are going on the fourth-grade camping trip next weekend. So we're going to visit Mrs. Taylor."

"Who's Mrs. Taylor?" Jessica asked, sitting down next to her mother on the couch.

"She's a friend of my family from way back," Mrs. Wakefield said. "When I was about your age, my sisters and I used to spend weekends with Mrs. Taylor. She lives in a very old house full of old things. We had wonderful adventures exploring every nook and cranny." Mrs. Wakefield laughed. "Mrs. Taylor wasn't always too happy about that."

"Mrs. Taylor must be really old if she was already grown-up when you were little," Elizabeth said.

Mrs. Wakefield smiled. "She is old—older

than even Grandma and Grandpa. And she has a mighty sharp tongue. So beware."

What will the twins discover in Mrs. Taylor's house? Find out in Sweet Valley Twins #41, **THE MISSING TEA SET.**

☎

1 (800) I LUV BKS!

If you'd like to hear more about your
favorite young adult novels and writers . . .
OR
If you'd like to tell us what you thought
of this book or other books
you've recently read . . .

CALL US at 1(800) I LUV BKS
[1(800)458-8257]

You'll hear a new message about books and
other interesting subjects each month.

**The call is free to you, but please get
your parents' permission first.**

Now You Can Buy

SWEET VALLEY HIGH

Dolls & Fashions

Available January 1993*
Wherever Toys Are Sold

NEW FROM

BAN DAI

SWEET VALLEY KIDS

Jessica and Elizabeth have had lots of adventures in *Sweet Valley High* and *Sweet Valley Twins*...now read about the twins at age seven! You'll love all the fun that comes with being seven—birthday parties, playing dress-up, class projects, putting on puppet shows and plays, losing a tooth, setting up lemonade stands, caring for animals and much more! It's all part of SWEET VALLEY KIDS. Read them all!

☐ JESSICA AND THE SPELLING-BEE SURPRISE #21	15917-8	$2.75
☐ SWEET VALLEY SLUMBER PARTY #22	15934-8	$2.99
☐ LILA'S HAUNTED HOUSE PARTY # 23	15919-4	$2.99
☐ COUSIN KELLY'S FAMILY SECRET # 24	15920-8	$2.99
☐ LEFT-OUT ELIZABETH # 25	15921-6	$2.99
☐ JESSICA'S SNOBBY CLUB # 26	15922-4	$2.99
☐ THE SWEET VALLEY CLEANUP TEAM # 27	15923-2	$2.99
☐ ELIZABETH MEETS HER HERO #28	15924-0	$2.99
☐ ANDY AND THE ALIEN # 29	15925-9	$2.99
☐ JESSICA'S UNBURIED TREASURE # 30	15926-7	$2.99
☐ ELIZABETH AND JESSICA RUN AWAY # 31	48004-9	$2.99
☐ LEFT BACK! #32	48005-7	$2.99
☐ CAROLINE'S HALLOWEEN SPELL # 33	48006-5	$2.99
☐ THE BEST THANKSGIVING EVER # 34	48007-3	$2.99
☐ ELIZABETH'S BROKEN ARM # 35	48009-X	$2.99
☐ ELIZABETH'S VIDEO FEVER # 36	48010-3	$2.99
☐ THE BIG RACE # 37	48011-1	$2.99
☐ GOODBYE, EVA? # 38	48012-X	$2.99
☐ ELLEN IS HOME ALONE # 39	48013-8	$2.99